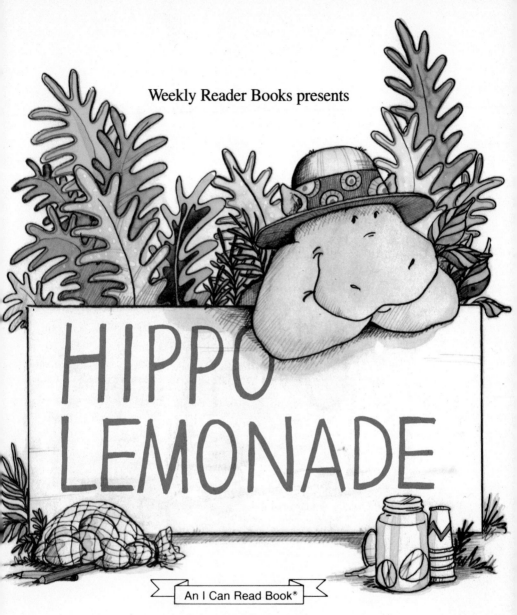

Weekly Reader Books presents

HIPPO LEMONADE

An I Can Read Book®

Mike Thaler
pictures by Maxie Chambliss

Harper & Row, Publishers

I Can Read Book is a registered trademark of
Harper & Row, Publishers, Inc.

Hippo Lemonade
Text copyright © 1986 by Mike Thaler
Illustrations copyright © 1986 by Maxie Chambliss
Printed in the U.S.A. All rights reserved.

Library of Congress Cataloging-in-Publication Data

Thaler, Mike, date
Hippo lemonade.

(An I can read book)
Summary: Hippo and his animal friends share a variety
of adventures including making a wish, selling lemonade,
and telling a scary story.
[1. Hippopotamus—Fiction.   2. Jungle animals—Fiction.
3. Animals—Fiction]   I. Chambliss, Maxie, ill.
II. Title.   III. Series.
PZ7.T3Hi 1986   [E]   85-45257
ISBN 0-06-026159-5
ISBN 0-06-026162-5 (lib. bdg.)

Designed by Al Cetta

For Nina—friend, editor, and nudge
M.T.

This one's for Elli - ♥ Max

Contents

Hippo Makes a Wish

Hippo opened his eyes.

"Today I would like

to make a wish," he said.

Hippo thought and thought.

6

But he could not think of anything

to wish for.

So he got out of the river

and went to see Snake.

"Snake," said Hippo,

"I would like to make a wish.

But I don't know what to wish for."

"Wish for bright colors, like mine,"

said Snake.

Hippo saw himself

with bright colors like Snake's.

8

"I don't think so," said Hippo.

And he went to see Monkey.

9

"Wish for a long tail like mine,"

said Monkey.

"Then we could swing

in the trees together."

Hippo saw himself
swinging in the trees.
"I don't think so," he said.
And he went to see Lion.

"Wish for a curly mane
like mine," said Lion.
Hippo saw himself
with a mane like Lion's.

"I don't think so," he said,
and he went to see Giraffe.

"You could see the tops of trees,"

said Giraffe,

"with a neck like mine."

Hippo saw himself

with a long neck like Giraffe's.

"I don't think so," said Hippo,

and he went to see Parrot.

"Feathers!" said Parrot.

"Wish for feathers."

Hippo saw himself

all covered with feathers.

"I don't think so," said Hippo,

and he went to see Elephant.

"I know!" said Elephant.

"Wish for a nose just like mine."

Hippo saw himself

with Elephant's nose.

"I don't think so," he said,

and he went back to the river.

He closed his eyes.

"What are you doing?" asked Mole.

"I am wishing," said Hippo.

"What are you wishing for?"

asked Mole.

"I am wishing to stay

just as I am," said Hippo.

Mole looked at Hippo.

Hippo looked at Mole.

Mole winked.

"Your wish has come true."

Hippo Lemonade

The sun was big in the sky.

"It's going to be a hot day,"

said Hippo.

18

He climbed out of the river
and walked to town.

He bought a straw hat,
some cups, and three lemons.

He found a jar, a box,
and a piece of cardboard.

Then he found

a shady spot by the river.

He filled the jar with water.

He squeezed the lemons

into the water.

Then he made a sign,

He put the sign on the box.

He put on his straw hat.

He was in business.

An hour passed.

Nobody came by.

Finally Snake wiggled up.

"What are you doing?" asked Snake.

"I am in business," said Hippo.

"Why?" asked Snake.

"To make money."

"How?" asked Snake.

"By selling lemonade.

Would you like some?" asked Hippo.

But Snake just wiggled off

down the road.

Another hour passed.

Nobody else came by.

Then Snake came wiggling back.

He had a box, a jar,

some cups, three lemons,

a straw hat and a sign.

He put his box next to Hippo's.

"What are you doing?" asked Hippo.

"I am in business," said Snake,

and he put on his straw hat.

"Oh!" said Hippo.

Snake filled his jar with water.

He squeezed the lemons

into the jar.

He put up his sign

in front of his box.

Hippo walked around and

looked at the sign.

Fresher
5¢
Lemonade

Hippo stood in front of Snake's sign.

He scratched his head.

Then he picked up his own sign

and wrote something on it.

Snake wiggled in front

and looked

at Hippo's sign.

Snake stood in front of Hippo's sign.

He scratched his head.

Then he picked up *his* sign

and wrote something on it.

Hippo walked around

and looked at the sign.

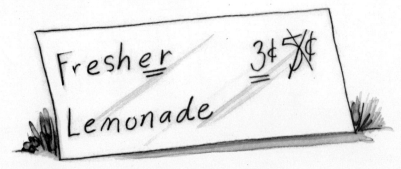

Hippo scratched his head.

Then he picked up *his* sign

and wrote something on it.

Snake wiggled in front

and looked at Hippo's sign.

It said

Snake picked up *his* sign and wrote

FRESHER LEMONADE 1¢.

Hippo picked up *his* sign and wrote

FRESH LEMONADE FREE.

Snake grabbed *his* sign and wrote

FRESHER LEMONADE FREE.

The two friends looked at each other.

They both were hot and tired.

"Would you like some lemonade?"

asked Hippo.

"Sure," said Snake.

"Would you like some of mine?"

"Sure," said Hippo.

So they sat down in the shade

and poured each other

a cup of lemonade.

"NOT BAD," said Hippo.

"NOT BAD," said Snake.

And that is how they spent the day,

sitting in the shade,

drinking lemonade.

The Scary Story

One night Hippo and his friends

decided to stay up all night.

They made a big campfire.

They toasted marshmallows.

They sang songs.

"Let's tell ghost stories," said Lion.

"No," said Mole, "fairy tales."

"Scary ghost stories," said Snake.

"No," said Mole, "happy fairy tales."

"Horrible, scary ghost stories,"

said Parrot.

"Okay," said Mole,

taking Hippo's hand.

"Who knows one?" asked Hippo.

"I do," said Snake.

"Okay," said Hippo,

holding Mole's hand. "Go ahead."

"One dark night in the jungle..."

began Snake.

"I'm scared," said Mole.

"You are such a sissy," said Lion.

"One dark night in the jungle,

almost as dark as tonight..."

said Snake.

Everyone looked around.

It *was* a dark night.

"Out of a deep, dark pool…"

Everyone moved closer together.

"…came a purple, slimy, one-eyed monster."

"Was it a right eye or a left eye?"

asked Hippo.

"It was a center eye,

red and bloodshot,

and looking for something to eat."

"What did it eat?" asked Mole,

hugging Hippo's hand.

"It ate moles and parrots,

and monkeys and lions,

and giraffes and elephants,

and hippos."

"Didn't it eat snakes?" asked Mole.

"No, it did not eat snakes,"

said Snake.

"Why not?" asked Parrot.

"Because this is my story,"

said Snake.

"I want it to eat snakes too,"

said Lion.

"Yeah," said everyone.

"Okay, okay, it ate snakes too.

"Well, anyway, it was *hungry*.

The slimy purple monster

crawled out of the dark pool

to look for someone to eat."

Everyone nodded.

"It crawled through the jungle

until it saw a light.

It was a campfire."

"Like ours?" asked Mole.

"Just like ours," said Snake.

"And around the campfire

sat a mole, a parrot, a lion,

a giraffe, an elephant,

and a hippo."

"What about a snake?" asked Mole.

"No snake," said Snake.

"The snake had gone home."

"I want the snake to be there,"

said Parrot.

"Yeah," said Lion.

"Yeah," said everyone else.

"Okay, okay,

the snake was there too.

"Anyway, the slimy purple creature

looked through its red bloodshot eye

and saw a parrot, a mole, a lion,

a giraffe, a hippo,

and an elephant."

"And a snake," said Mole.

"And a snake,

all sitting around a campfire.

Its purple stomach grumbled,

and it licked its yellow teeth."

"What was that?" cried Mole.

"What!" said Snake.

"I heard a noise," said Mole.

Everyone looked out

into the dark jungle.

They waited

and listened.

But they did not hear anything.

"Anyway…" said Snake,

"it licked its yellow teeth and

crawled closer to the campfire."

"What was that?" cried Mole.

"What?" shouted Snake.

"A noise! I heard a noise,"

said Mole.

Everyone listened.

But the dark jungle was silent.

"It licked its yellow teeth

and crawled closer, and closer,

and closer, and…"

Mole screamed.

Lion and Parrot,

Hippo, Elephant, and Giraffe

jumped up.

"What is it?" Snake swallowed hard.

"I saw something move," said Mole.

"WHAT?" yelled Snake,

hiding behind Hippo.

"I don't know," said Mole.

They all huddled together,

close to the fire.

"How does your story *end*?"

asked Lion.

"Well," said Snake,

looking out into the dark jungle,

"the monster decides

it is not really hungry,

and it goes away

and never comes back."

They all sighed.

"That was a good story," said Monkey.

"It was not so scary," said Lion.

He let go of  Elephant's nose.

"Can someone tell a fairy tale now?"

asked Mole.

"Sure," said Snake,

"I know a good one."

"Okay," said everyone,

sitting down again.

Snake smiled and began,

"One dark night in the jungle..."

Clouds

One morning, Hippo woke up.

He felt like being alone.

He rolled over in the river.

He floated on his back.

The clouds floated above him.

Hippo smiled.

One big fluffy cloud

looked like Elephant.

It even had a long fluffy nose.

"Wow!" said Hippo.

Another cloud looked like Giraffe.

It had a long skinny neck

and tall cloud legs.

The cloud beside it had
a white fluffy mane.
Slowly it opened its mouth
in a silent roar.

High above

swung a little Monkey cloud.

A Snake cloud wiggled by.

Then came a tiny fluff.

It looked like Mole.

Hippo began to feel lonely.

He rolled over.

He swam to the shore.

He got out of the river and looked up.

"Good-bye, clouds," he said.

And he ran to find his friends.